This Little Tiger book belongs to:

_____

_____

_____

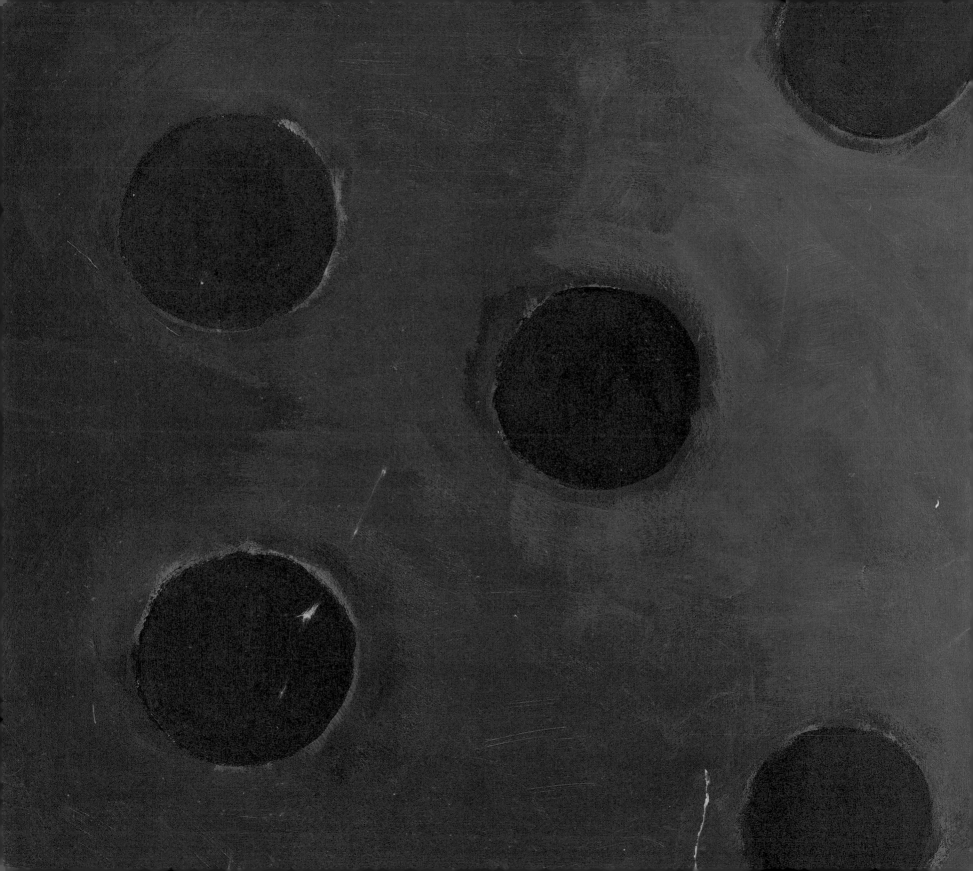

For Andrea & Claudia
— I F

For Mum & Dad, who helped
— J T

LITTLE TIGER PRESS
1 The Coda Centre, 189 Munster Road, London SW6 6AW
www.littletiger.co.uk

First published in Great Britain 1999
This edition published 2016

A CIP catalogue record for this book is
available from the British Library

All rights reserved • ISBN 978-1-84869-384-5

Printed in China • LTP/1900/1740/1216

2 4 6 8 10 9 7 5 3

The Very Lazy Ladybird

by Isobel Finn & Jack Tickle

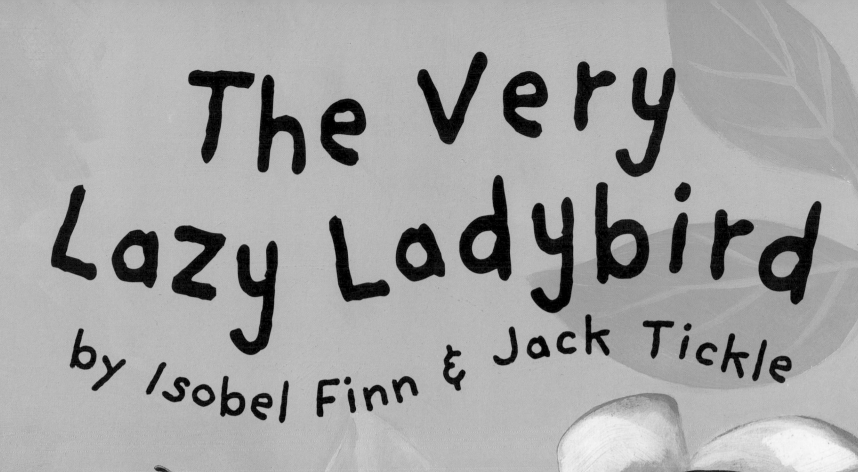

LITTLE TIGER PRESS
London

This is the story of
a very lazy ladybird.

...and all night.

And because she slept
all day and all night,
this lazy ladybird didn't
know how to fly.

One day the lazy
ladybird wanted to
sleep somewhere else.
But what could she do
if she couldn't fly?

Then the lazy
ladybird had
a very good
idea.

When a kangaroo bounded by . . .

...she hopped into her pouch.

But the kangaroo liked to

JUMP!

"I can't sleep in here,"
cried the lazy ladybird.
"It's far too bumpy."

So when a tiger padded by . . .

But the tiger liked to

ROAR!

"I can't sleep here,"
said the lazy ladybird.
"It's far too noisy."

So when a crocodile swam by . . .

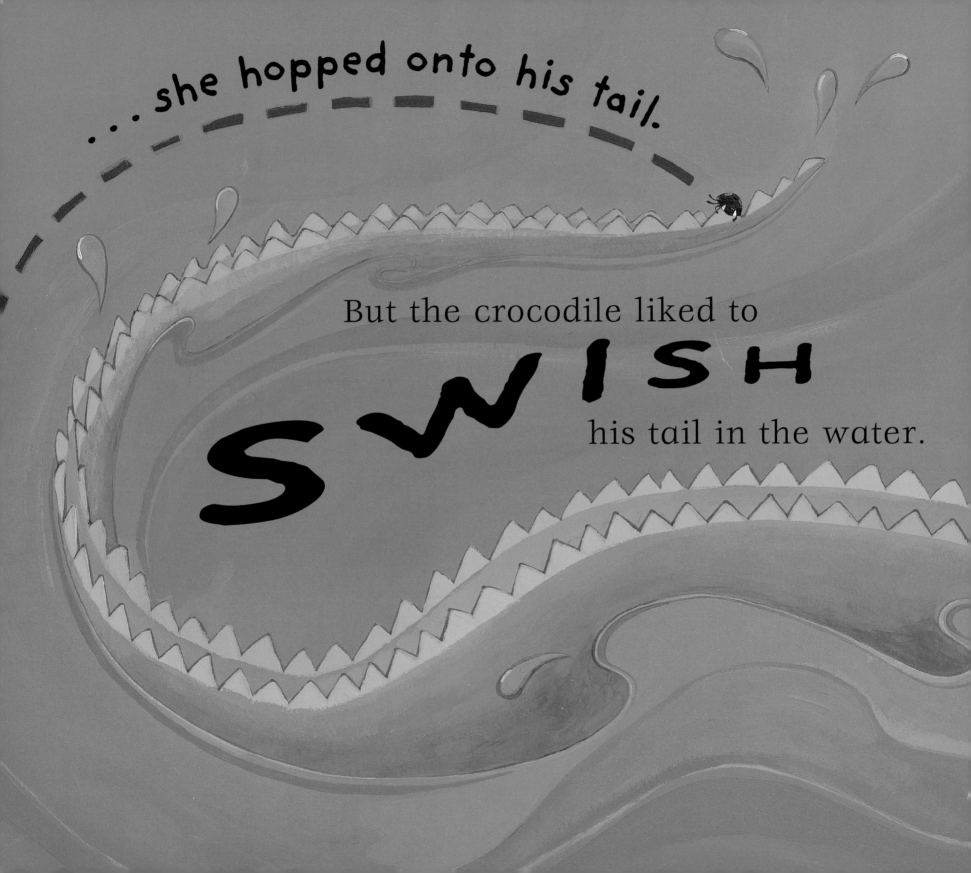

...she hopped onto his tail.

But the crocodile liked to

SWISH

his tail in the water.

"I can't sleep here,"
said the lazy ladybird.
"I'll fall into the river!"

So when a monkey swung by . . .

...she hopped onto her head.

But the monkey liked to

SWING

from branch to branch.

"I can't sleep here,"
said the lazy ladybird.
"I'm feeling dizzy."

So when a bear ambled by . . .

"I can't sleep here,"
said the lazy ladybird.
"He'll never sit still."

So when a tortoise plodded by . . .

...she hopped onto her shell.

But the tortoise liked to
S N O O Z E
in the sun.
"I can't sleep here,"
said the lazy ladybird.
"It's far too hot."

But at that very moment . . .

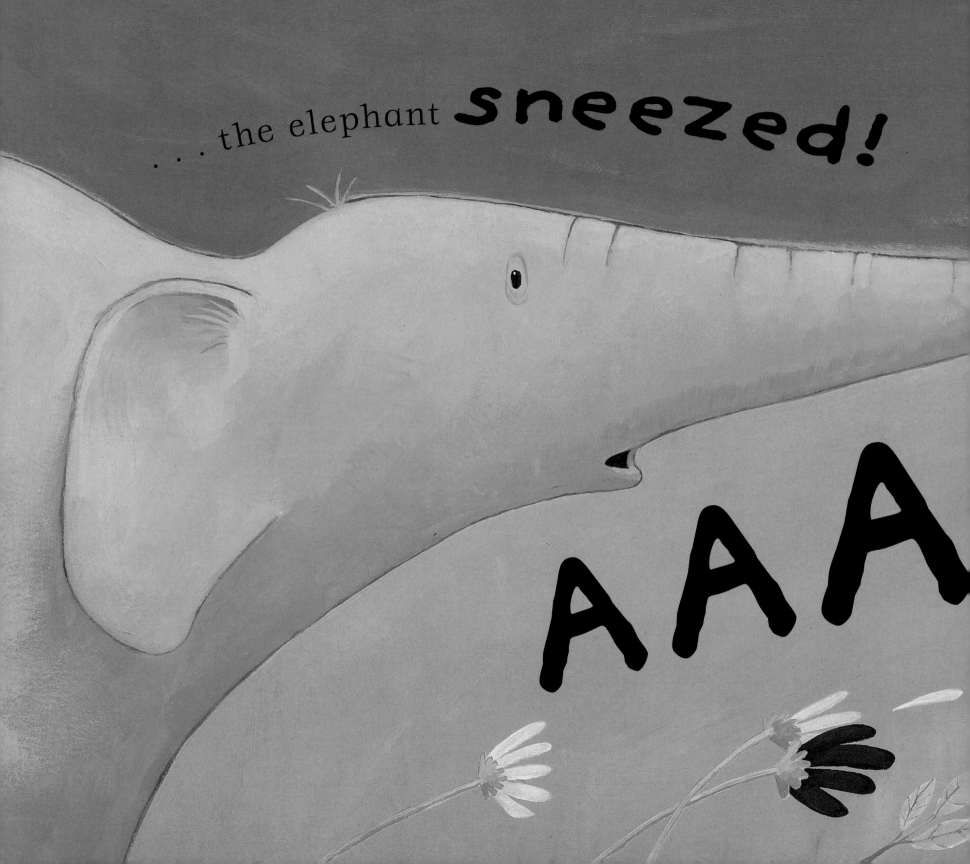

CHOOo!

and poor old lazy ladybird . . .

. . . had to fly
at last!

Aaaaaaaaahhh

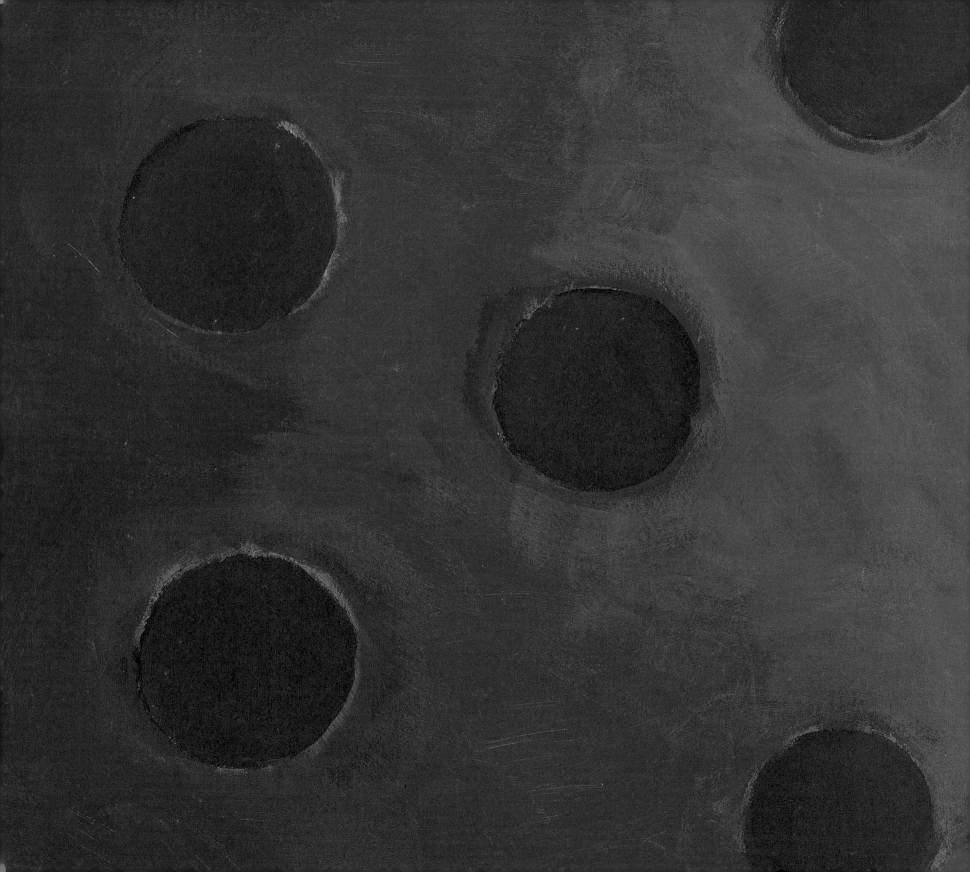

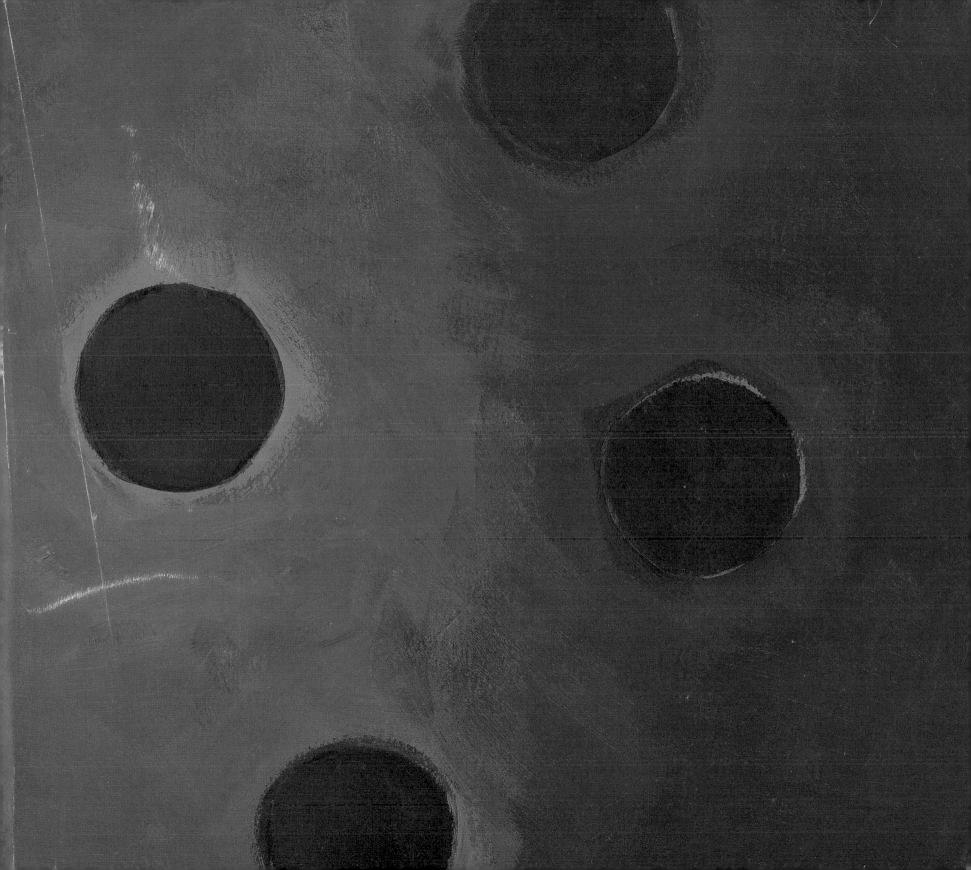

CD track 1 – complete story with original music and sound effects
CD track 2 – story with page turn pings encourages learner readers to join in

Running time – over 15 mins • Produced by The Complete Works, Warwickshire CV31 1JP,
in conjunction with Stationhouse • Music composed by Jim Betteridge and Sam Park

Visit our website www.littletiger.co.uk for details of other Little Tiger Picture Book
and CD Sets, plus our full catalogue of novelty, board and picture books.